D1410084

Hello, Tiger!

Aimee Aryal

Illustrated by Joni Graybill

www.mascotbooks.com

It was a beautiful fall day at
Clemson University.

The Tiger was on his way to
Memorial Stadium to watch
a football game.

He passed by Bowman Field and walked
up to the statue of Thomas Green Clemson
in front of Tillman Hall.

A professor walking by waved,
"Hello, Tiger!"

The Tiger went by the Amphitheater
on his way to Cooper Library.

Some students studying there said,
"Hello, Tiger!"

The Tiger walked over to Fort Hill.

A family visiting Calhoun Mansion
said, "Hello, Tiger!"

The Tiger went to Littlejohn Coliseum
and stopped at the Tiger Statue.

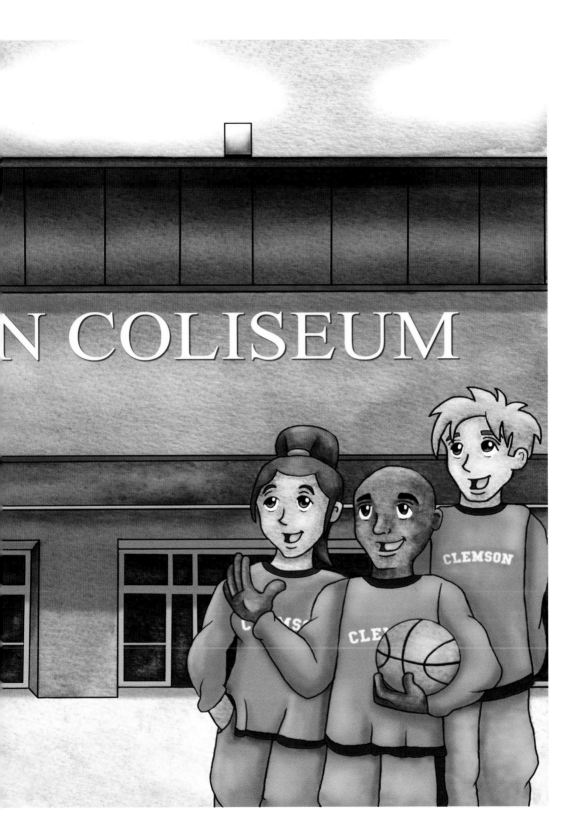

Some basketball players standing
nearby yelled, "Hello, Tiger!"

It was almost time for the football game.
As the Tiger walked to the stadium,
he passed by some alumni.

The alumni remembered the Tiger from
their days at Clemson University.
They said, "Hello, again, Tiger!"

Finally, the Tiger arrived at
"Death Valley."

He watched the football players touch
Howard's Rock as they ran down the hill.
The crowd cheered, "Go, Tigers!"

The Tiger watched the game from the sidelines and cheered for the team.

The Tigers scored six points!
The quarterback shouted,
"Touchdown, Tiger!"

At halftime, the Tiger Band
performed on the field.

The Tiger and the crowd
listened to "Tiger Rag."

The Clemson Tigers won
the football game!

The Tiger gave the coach a high-five.
The coach said,
"Great game, Tiger!"

After the football game, the Tiger
was tired. It had been a long day
at Clemson University.

He walked home and climbed into bed.

Good night, Tiger.

For Anna and Maya,
and all of the Tiger's little fans. ~ AA

To Amy, the Tiger in the family,
for always being my inspiration. ~ JG

For more information about our products,
please visit us online at www.mascotbooks.com.

Copyright © 2004, Mascot Books, Inc. All rights reserved.
No part of this book may be reproduced by any means.

For more information, please contact Mascot Books,
P.O. Box 220157, Chantilly, VA 20153-0157

CLEMSON UNIVERSITY, CLEMSON, TIGERS, CLEMSON TIGERS, DEATH VALLEY, and
HOWARD'S ROCK are trademarks or registered trademarks of
Clemson University and are used under license.

ISBN: 1-932888-25-X

Printed in the United States.

www.mascotbooks.com